DISNEY
THE
ARISTOCATS

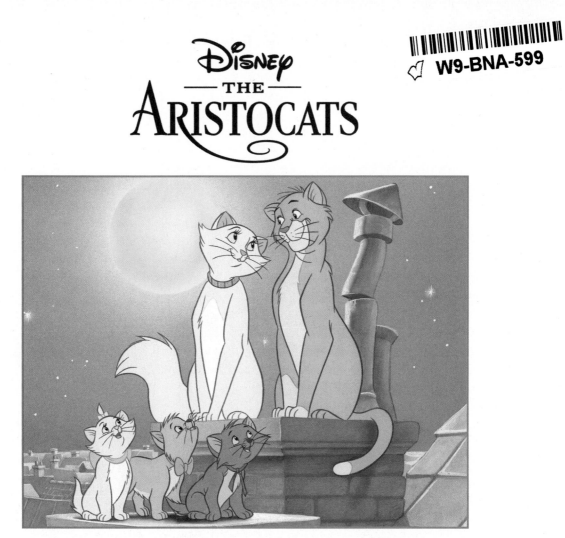

Duchess and her three kittens—no ordinary cats—
find their way home with the help of Thomas—
one extraordinary alley cat.

The Aristocats is based on the book by Thomas Rowe.

Long ago, in the beautiful city of Paris, lived a kind, wealthy lady and her family of cats. There was Duchess, the mother cat, and her three darling (and sometimes mischievous) kittens: Toulouse, Marie, and Berlioz.

Madame Adelaide Bonfamille loved sharing her beautiful home with Duchess and the kittens. They were served the very best food on silver trays. They even slept in their own canopied bed in Madame's room.

These were no ordinary cats—they were *Aristocats*.

Toulouse was a talented painter. Berlioz liked to play the grand piano. And Marie planned to be a great singer someday.

Madame loved her cats so much that she wanted to make sure they would enjoy the good life even after she was gone. So one day she asked her lawyer to visit.

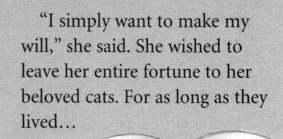

"I simply want to make my will," she said. She wished to leave her entire fortune to her beloved cats. For as long as they lived…

…they would be cared for by Edgar, her faithful butler. When the cats were gone, her fortune would go to him.

Downstairs, Edgar the butler was listening to every word through a speaking tube in his room. He was quite distressed that he would have to wait for the cats to die before he got any money.

"Cats inherit first, and I come after the cats!" he muttered. "It's not fair!"

That evening, Edgar stirred sleeping pills into the cats' milk.

"Your favorite dish," said Edgar, setting down the bowls. "Prepared a very special way—*crème de la crème à la Edgar!*"

The cats and their friend, Roquefort the mouse, lapped up every drop. The cats just managed to stagger to their basket before they fell into a deep sleep.

As soon as Madame was in bed, Edgar sneaked the cats out of the house to take them to the countryside—and leave them!

But Edgar's plans were spoiled!

Just outside Paris, two dogs jumped out, barking and snarling, giving Edgar a terrible fright. As he swerved, the basket of sleeping cats tumbled out of the sidecar, and Edgar sped off, leaving the basket—and the cats—behind

When the cats awoke, they found themselves in the rain near a bridge.

How had they gotten there? they wondered.

Toulouse had had a dream. "Edgar was in it," he said. "And we were all riding and bouncing along…" Then he looked around him and added. "It *wasn't* a dream. Edgar did this to us!"

"What's going to happen to us?" asked Berlioz.

Duchess sighed. "Poor Madame. She'll be worried when she finds us gone."

The next morning, the cats crawled out of the basket. As Duchess wondered what to do, an alley cat strolled by and introduced himself as Abraham DeLacey Giuseppe Casey Thomas O'Malley the alley cat.

He gave a friendly smile when he saw Duchess and the kittens, and they smiled back at him.

When they told O'Malley they were lost, he offered to help them get back to Paris.

Duchess and the kittens were very grateful for his help.

"Poor Madame—in that big mansion, all alone," said Duchess softly. "She'd always say that we were the greatest treasure she could own."

All that day and into the night, the little band of cats—Duchess, Marie, Toulouse, Berlioz, and O'Malley— trudged on toward Paris. Duchess and the kittens were used to riding in carriages, not walking along country roads and across rooftops!

By the time they reached Paris, they were exhausted.

"Mama, I'm tired," whined Marie.

"Me, too. And my feet hurt," said Berlioz.

"I bet we walked a hundred miles," sighed Toulouse.

It was still a long way to
Madame's mansion, so O'Malley
invited Duchess and the kittens
to stay at his house.

But when they got there, they
found that O'Malley already had
visitors. A group of alley cats, led
by O'Malley's friend, Scat Cat, were
playing jazz music.

The whole building was swinging
to the beat!

The kittens forgot about being tired and joined in the fun. Berlioz helped play the old piano, Toulouse kept time to the music, and Marie sang at the top of her voice.

Even Duchess couldn't resist joining in. She and O'Malley danced happily until midnight.

Later, after the jazz band left, O'Malley and Duchess sat together in the moonlight, looking over the rooftops of Paris.

O'Malley told Duchess that he wished she and the kittens could stay. "Ya know… they need a… well… you know, a sort of a… well, a father around."

Duchess wished she could stay, too. But she had to think of Madame.

"I'm sorry, my dear," she told O'Malley sadly. "We just have to go home tomorrow."

The next morning, O'Malley escorted Duchess and the kittens home to Madame's house.

As the kittens scampered ahead, Duchess and O'Malley stopped at the gate to say good-bye.

"I'll never forget you, Thomas O'Malley," said Duchess fondly.

Meanwhile, Edgar was in the kitchen, when suddenly, he heard the sound of kittens meowing at the front door!

"It can't be them!" he exclaimed.

As the cats came through the door, a sack came down over their heads. "You came back!" Edgar muttered. "It just isn't fair."

Edgar took the sack out to the barn and put it in a trunk that was being sent to Timbuktu!

But Roquefort the mouse saw
everything. He dashed outside to
tell O'Malley.

"Duchess and the kittens
in trouble?" said O'Malley.
"Look—you go get Scat Cat
and the alley cats!" He told
Roquefort how to find them,
and then he set off for the
mansion.

By the time Roquefort
returned, Edgar had trapped
O'Malley in the barn with
a pitchfork. The alley cats
stormed in, hissing, biting,
and scratching!

While the cats dealt with Edgar, O'Malley helped Duchess and the kittens out of the trunk—and then the horse kicked Edgar into that stuffy trunk—just as the deliverymen arrived!

Now *Edgar* was on his way to Timbuktu!

Madame Bonfamille was thrilled to have Duchess and the kittens back. She was also delighted to meet O'Malley.

"I think this young man is very handsome," she said to Duchess. "Shall we keep him in the family?"

Madame decided to set up a home for all the homeless alley cats of Paris. From then on, all cats would be treated as special, wonderful *Aristocats*.